THE CURSED COLONY

AF080961

Orange Books Publication

1st Floor, Rajhans Arcade, Mall Road, Kohka, Bhilai, Chhattisgarh 490020

Website: **www.orangebooks.in**

© **Copyright, 2025, Author**

All rights reserved. No part of this book may be reproduced, stored in a retrieval system, or transmitted, in any form by any means, electronic, mechanical, magnetic, optical, chemical, manual, photocopying, recording or otherwise, without the prior written consent of its writer.

First Edition, 2025

ISBN: 978-93-6554-879-2

THE CURSED COLONY

SHAURYA GUPTA

Orange Books Publication
www.orangebooks.in

Index

Chapter 1	1
Chapter 2	3
Chapter 3	9
Chapter 4	12
Chapter 5	13
Chapter 6	15
Chapter 7	17
Chapter 8	18
Chapter 9	20
Chapter 10	22
Chapter 11	24
Chapter 12	26
Chapter 13	27
Chapter 14	29
Chapter 15	30
Chapter 16	31
Chapter 17	32
Chapter 18	35
Chapter 19	38
Chapter 20	39
Chapter 21	41
Chapter 22	43
Chapter 23	44

Chapter 24	46
Chapter 25	48
Chapter 26	51
Chapter 27	53
Chapter 28	56
Chapter 29	58
Chapter 30	61
Chapter 31	63
Chapter 32	64
Chapter 33	66
Chapter 34	70
Chapter 35	75
Chapter 36	76
The Story Of The Colony	79

Chapter 1

Alarm Ringing…

Ringing Ringing

Ringing Ringing Ringing Ringing

Chetan-Huhhhh.

Chetan woke up.

It was the time of summer holidays.

Chetan woke up at 11 AM.

Chetan- Mata Shri, Mata Shri.

Sushma- Yes Beta,

Chetan- I am hungry.

Sushma- First go and brush and then come downstairs.

Chetan- Ok Mata Shri

Chetan brushed and went down to have breakfast. The time was around 11:30 AM.

Chetan- Mata Shri what is there for breakfast ?

Sushma- Breakfast? Have you seen the time, it's already 11:33 AM.

Chetan- Sorry, Mata Shri

Sushma- I know your Summer Vacations are going on but from tomorrow you will have to wake up before 10 AM or you will not get any breakfast!!!

Chetan- Ok Mata Shri

Chetan lives with his parents and grandparents in his house. His grandparents lived on the ground floor and his parents and he had their room on the first floor.

Chapter 2

It was around 4:32 in the evening suddenly Chetan's Phone Rang.

जय हनुमान ज्ञान गुण सागर

(Hanuman Chalisa)

Then Chetan Answered the call.

Rohan- Hi Bro, How are you?

Chetan- Good Bro What about you?

Rohan- I am Good. Wanna go on a Scooter Ride?

Chetan- I am in, let's go.

Rohan Arrived at Chetan's House

Rohan- Hi Bro, I am very Bored.

Chetan- Hi same here. Let's go and eat something

Rohan- ok. Do you have some money??

Chetan- Yeah.

Rohan- Ok. Let's go.

Rohan is Chetan's best friend. Chetan mounted on Rohan's Activa and they went to eat something Chetan and Rohan arrived at a road side fast food cart.

Vendor- Good Evening sir! What would you like to have?

Rohan- 1 Full Plate momos and 1 Full Plate Spring Rolls. How much time it will take??

Vendor- Sir it will take around 15 Mins.

Rohan- Ok. And How Much??

Vendor- 200 Sir.

Rohan- Ok. Do you have change??

Vendor- Yes sir.

Rohan- Ok. Take 500 and give the change

Vendor- Take it, sir.

Rohan- Thank You.

Chetan- Rohan wanna go to the Mandir (Temple) after eating?

Rohan- Sure why not.

Chetan's Phone Rang

जय हनुमान ज्ञान गुण सागर।

जय कपीस तिहुं लोक उजागर॥

रामदूत अतुलित बल धामा।

अंजनि-पुत्र पवनसुत नामा॥

(Hanuman Chalisa)

Chetan- Hello Mata Shri.

Sushma- Beta Where are you?

Chetan- I'm with Rohan.

Sushma- Ok. When you will come home?

Chetan- In 45 mins to 1 hour.

Sushma - ok Beta. Bye.

Chetan- Bye Mata Shri.

Chetan disconnected the call.

Rohan - What was your mom saying ?

Chetan- Nothing she was just asking where I am.

Rohan – ok.

Vendor- Sir, Your order is ready.

Rohan- come Chetan let's eat.

Rohan and Chetan ate the food and sat on the scooter.

Rohan- Bro what should we do now?

Chetan- Idk bro.

Rohan- I have a plan.

Chetan- What?

Rohan- Let's go on a geri in Ria's colony, I haven't seen her for many days.

Chetan- No bro this is a very risky idea.

Rohan- Please bro, don't you know she's, my crush?

Chetan- Ok bro.

Rohan and Chetan were on the way to Ria's colony (Rohan's Crush) when a black cat crossed their way.

Rohan- Now we have to take another way. Bruh!

Chetan- Why?

Rohan- Didn't you see that a black cat crossed our way???

Chetan- So What ?

Rohan- Don't you know it is ominous??

Chetan- Who cares?

Rohan- WHAT?

Chetan- I don't believe in these types of myths, ghosts, etc.

Rohan- Why??

Chetan- I don't believe, I believe in Hanuman ji.

Rohan- You believe gods exist?

Chetan- Yes, I do.

Rohan- Then, believe me, these things also exist
Chetan- Whatever!

Rohan took another way and after some time they reached Ria's colony.

Rohan- Bro I am nervous.

Chetan- Why bro, we are here just for a geri.

They passed 2-3 times in front of her house.

Chetan- Bro I think we should go now.

Rohan- Yes Let's go.

Rohan dropped Chetan home

Chetan- Bye Bro.

Rohan- Bye.

After saying bye to Rohan, Chetan entered his house.

Chetan- Mata Shri (Mom) I'm home.

Sushma- Beta (Son) you wanna eat something?

Chetan- No Mata Shri (Mom).

Sushma- Ok.

Chetan- By The Way what is there for Dinner?

Sushma- Kadhai Paneer with Roti.

Chetan- Ok.

Then Chetan went to his room.

Chapter 3

Chetan Heard Listened The Door Open, it was his father and grandfather. They came back from their work.

Manohar- Chetan Beta come downstairs.

Chetan- Coming Pita Shri.

Chetan Left his room and went downstairs.

Chetan - Yes pita shri.

Manohar - You remember your Ashok uncle?

Chetan- No Pita Shri.

Manohar- Oh! I remember you were very small when you met him and then he went Abroad. Now he is back to India and he has bought a new house here in India and tomorrow we have to go to his place for a party.

Chetan- Wow! Pita shri that's awesome.

Sushma - What are you both talking about?

Chetan- Mata shri tomorrow we are going for a partyyyyy !!

Sushma- Manohar whose party is he talking about?

Manohar - You remember Ashok ?

Sushma- Yes - yes, he shifted abroad a few years back.

Manohar - Ya, he came back and he has bought a new house. Tomorrow, we have to go to his place.

Sushma- Oh, now I have to look what I have to wear. First let's have dinner. Chetan go and call Dadi.

Chetan Entered his Grandparents room.

Chetan- Dadi let's have dinner.

Grandmother - Coming Beta.

Chetan and his Grandmother Left The Room and joined others for dinner.

After Dinner everyone went to their rooms.

Sushma- What Should I wear tomorrow ?

Manohar- You can decide that in the morning also let's sleep now.

Sushma- Ok Manohar, but at what time do we have to go tomorrow?

Manohar- We have to reach there at 8 in the evening. We will leave at 7.

Sushma - Ok, you know where the house is ?

Manohar - No, but I have the location.

Sushma- Ok, that's nice, Good Night.

Manohar- Good Night.

Chapter 4

(Wakes up early in the morning)

Chetan - What a pleasant morning. I think I should go for a Morning Walk.

Chetan got up from his bed, put on his shoes and went downstairs.

Chetan - Good Morning Dada. (Grandfather)

Grandfather- Good Morning beta (Son). You got up early today, are you going somewhere ?

Chetan- No No, I woke up early so I thought I should go for a morning walk.

Grandfather- That's good for your health too.

Chetan- Yes, Bye Dada. (grandfather)

Grandfather- Bye Beta. (Son)

Chetan Left his home and went for a morning walk.

Chapter 5

After the Morning Chetan came back home and his mother was shocked.

Sushma- Chetan how are you awake so early??

Chetan- I don't know Mata Shri. (Mom)

Sushma- Whatever, go and sit I am bringing your breakfast.

Chetan- Ok Mata Shri. (Mom)

Chetan sat on the chair and Sushma served him breakfast.

After breakfast, Chetan went to his room.

Chetan- I am so bored. Let me play some games on PS4.

After playing when Chetan saw the time it was 3:30 PM.

Chetan- OMG I have been playing for a long time.

Sushma entered Chetan's room.

Sushma- Chetan beta I am going to the salon.

Chetan- Ok Mata Shri. (Mom)

Sushma exited Chetan's room Chetan made a call to Rohan.

Chetan- Hi Rohan how are you?

Rohan- Hi Bro, I am good what about you?

Chetan- I am also good and bored also.

Rohan- Same here wanna play BGMI?

Chetan- Ya sure, come online.

Rohan- Coming.

Chapter 6

Sushma came back from the salon and found that Chetan was busy playing BGMI with Rohan.

Sushma- Chetan you are still playing games?

Chetan- Mata Shri (Mom) back so soon ??

Sushma- Yes and it's 6:00 PM.

Chetan- I was going to close the game.

Sushma- I don't want any excuse to close it now.

Chetan- Ok Mata Shri (Mom)

Sushma- And get ready your Dad is almost home, we have to leave at 7PM.

Chetan- OK Mata Shri. (Mom)

Chetan got ready and went to his parent's room.

Chetan- Mata Shri (Mom) I'm ready.

Sushma- Perfect, now call and ask your Dad where he is.

Chetan- Ok Mata Shri. (Mom)

Chetan made a call to his father.

Chetan- Pita Shri (Dad) where are you?

Manohar- Beta (Son) I'm parking the car outside our home.

Chetan- Ok Pita Shri. (Dad)

Chetan- Pita Shri (Dad) is parking the car outside Mata Shri (Mom).

Sushma- Ok Beta. (son)

Manohar entered the room.

Manohar- I'm here.

Sushma- You took a lot of time.

Manohar- I'm going to get ready quickly just give me 5mins.

Chapter 7

After getting ready Manohar came into the room.

Manohar- I'm ready, let's go.

Sushma- Where has Ashok bought his new house?

Manohar- I don't know, he said he has taken the house in a colony. Don't worry I have the location.

Sushma- Ok. Let's go.

Manohar, Chetan, and Sushma exited their house and entered the car.

Manohar opened the location on his phone, started the car, and started following the location.

Chapter 8

Manohar stopped the car and saw that the gate of the colony was rusted and was not in shape, every house in the colony was in a very bad condition.

Manohar- We are at the location.

Sushma- Are you sure?

Manohar- According to maps we are at the correct location.

Sushma- Sometimes the maps take you to the wrong location. You must call Ashok.

Manohar- Ok.

Manohar made a call to Ashok.

Manohar- Hi Ashok.

Ashok- Hi, where are you? I am waiting eagerly for you.

Manohar- I am at the location that you had sent to me but I think I am lost.

Ashok- Is there a rusted Gate in front of you.

Manohar- Yes.

Ashok- Then just come in.

Manohar- Ok.

Manohar took his car inside the colony.

Manohar- I am inside the colony; now where do I have to come ?

Ashok- Wait I am coming outside.

Manohar- Ok.

Ashok- I'm outside.

Manohar- Ya, I spotted you.

Chapter 9

Ashok- Namaste. (Hello)

Bhabhi ji- Hello Beta.

Sushma- Namaste.

Chetan- Namaste Uncle.

Manohar- Ashok, you forgot me.

Ashok-No- No, I've not forgotten you I was just trolling you, hahahaha.

Ashok hugged Manohar.

Ashok- Let's go inside.

Everyone went inside.

Manohar- Wow your house is nice. But why did you buy a house here ?

Ashok- I got it a very cheap.

Manohar- How much?

Ashok- I got it for just 45 lakhs .

Manohar- You got a great deal, but isn't the location very odd?

Ashok- Ya, I know but it was such a good deal that I was unable to ignore it.

Manohar- Ok.

Ashok- Let's have dinner.

Manohar- Ok.

They all went to have dinner.

Chapter 10

After dinner, they all sat on the couch and started talking. But unexpectedly there was a noise outside so Ashok went outside to check.

Sushma- Manohar I am not getting good vibes. We are in the middle of nowhere and that noise. I am scared.

Chetan- Mata Shri (Mom) don't worry everything is ok.

Manohar- Yes Sushma don't worry. Let Ashok come back.

Sushma- Ok.

Ashok came back and suddenly it started raining, and there were sounds of thunder.

Ashok- Everything is fine outside.

Sushma whispered to Manohar.

Sushma- Manohar isn't Ashok behaving somewhat weirdly.

Manohar- Yes, I also felt the same.

Sushma- I think we should leave now.

Manohar- Ashok I think we should leave now, it is getting late.

Ashok said in a weird voice.

Ashok- Why are you leaving so early?

The moment Ashok said this all the lights of the house started flickering.

Chapter 11

Everyone started screaming and the lights started flickering more.

Suddenly someone's phone rang

जय हनुमान ज्ञान गुण सागर ।

जय कपीस तिहुं लोक उजागर ॥

रामदूत अतुलित बल धामा ।

अंजनि-पुत्र पवनसुत नामा ॥

After that everything stopped there was no flickering of lights Ashok Fainted on the couch and everyone was shocked.

Manohar- What did just happen? Sushma are you ok? Chetan where are you?

Chetan- Pita Shri (Dad) I'm all right.

Sushma- I'm also ok.

Manohar- Ashok! Ashok! he is not getting up. Sushma please get some water.

Sushma brought some water and Manohar splashed it on Ashok's face Ashok woke up.

Ashok- where am I

Manohar- You are at your home in India.

Ashok- Oh I remember I went outside to check but after that, I don't remember what happened.

Manohar- Ashok something is not right here, I think we should leave.

Manohar picked up the car keys and approached the door with Sushma, Chetan and Ashok

Chapter 12

When Manohar Tried to open the door, it was not opening, he tried and tried and tried but nothing helped.

Manohar- I think we are stuck here, Chetan please try calling the police.

Chetan- Ok Pita Shri. (Dad)

Sushma- Manohar I'm afraid, what now?

Manohar- Don't worry Sushma.

Chetan- Pita Shri (Dad) my phone's battery is dead please give me your phone.

Manohar gave his phone to Chetan.

Chetan- Pita Shri (Dad) Network is not available.

Manohar- We have to find another way to escape.

Chapter 13

Everyone was terrified and suddenly a sound came

Unknown sound- You all should not have come here. You all made a big mistake.

Manohar- From where is this sound coming from ?

Ashok- I don't know.

Chetan- Pita Shri (Dad) I'm afraid.

Sushma- Do something

Unknown Sound- You all should not have come here. You all made a big mistake.

Manohar- Whoever you are, let us go we will leave and will never come back here.

Unknown Sound- What do you think I am, You all are now trapped here, hahahahahahaha.

Manohar- We all are extremely sorry, please let us go

All lights started flickering again, and everyone scattered and started finding ways to escape but suddenly flickering stopped.

Chetan- (Mom) Pita Shri (Dad) flickering stopped.

After saying this Chetan started finding his parents but no one was there.

Chetan- The door is open I think everyone went outside.

When Chetan stepped outside there was no one there, their car was fully destroyed and everywhere there was just blood.

Chetan- What is this, is anyone here ??, Help, Help, Help.

Chetan started walking in the hope to find someone.

Chapter 14

The flickering stopped and Sushma felt a relief.

Sushma- Chetan, Manohar lights stopped flickering let's meet in the lobby.

Sushma reached the lobby and waited for a while but no one came.

Sushma- Why is no one coming, I think I should go and check outside.

Sushma tried to open the door and she was successful in her attempt.

Sushma- Yessss finally the door opened.

When Sushma stepped out of the door, she found herself in front of the same door, she felt weird she entered the door again but found herself in the same place. Sushma was trapped in a loop

Chapter 15

On the other hand, when the flickering stopped Manohar and Ashok met in the lobby and started looking for Sushma and Chetan. They both tried to open the door and were successful in their attempt

Manohar- Ashok let's go outside and look for them.
Ashok - Ok let's go.

They both went outside but found themselves in a restaurant

Manohar- What place is this? Ashok- Let's go and ask the waiter.

Manohar- Ok.

Ashok- Excuse me.

Waiter- Sir please have a seat first.

Manohar and Ashok sat on the chairs and suddenly they got handcuffed on the chair and then they found themselves in the same house.

Chapter 16

Chetan was walking in the hope to find someone suddenly he found a door.

Chetan- Finally after hours of walking I found something.

Chetan opened and entered the door But he found himself in the same house..

Chetan- What's happening? In the same house? Hello! Hello! Anyone here? Help me!

Chetan felt tired and sat on the sofa in the hope that someone would come but the walls started to become red with blood.

Chetan- Help me, please someone help me!

Unknown Sound - No one will come here now, hahahahahaha. You are trapped now.

Chapter 17

Dug Dug Dug

A police man was passing from the road.

Policeman- Huh! My job is very hard, I have to pass from this scary colony alone.

While passing he spotted Manohar's car in the colony.

Policeman- A car? This is an abandoned colony. Why is there a car here?

Policeman took out his walkie -talkie and connected to the control room.

Policeman- Hello! Hello control room, am I audible?

Control Room- Yes.

Policeman- I was going to report to my night duty but on the way I saw a car in the abandoned colony, from many years this has been abandoned and no one has lived here.

Control Room- This is a matter of concern, you go and check and we will sending a backup.

Policeman- Ok.

Control Room- Send us your location.

Policeman- Ok.

The Policeman took his bag and torch and entered the colony.

After a little walk, he reached the car and opened the door of the house.

The moment he entered the house he was shocked, he saw 4 people lying on the floor. He checked them and found that they all were alive, when he saw their eyes they s were all white as if someone had possessed them. He immediately reported to the Control room.

Policeman- Control Room! Control Room! I need backup and an ambulance fast here are 4 people lying, send an ambulance fasttt !

Control Room- Ok, Ok Ambulance and backup are on its way till then try to wake them up.

Policeman- Ok.

The Policeman took out a water bottle from his bag and sprinkled some water on Chetan's face.

Policeman- Beta, Beta are you ok?

Chetan- Where am I? Who are you? What have you done to my parents and uncle? Mata Shri (Mom) Pita Shri (Dad) are you ok? Wake up.

Policeman- Beta relax they just fainted they will wake up, an ambulance is on its way.

The Policeman-then sprinkled water on Manohar, Sushma, and Ashok's face. Manohar and Sushma woke up but Ashok was not getting up, the ambulance reached outside the house and took everyone to the hospital, Police sealed the house and the colony for investigation.

Chapter 18

Policeman went to interrogate Ashok in the Hospital

Policeman- Mr. Ashok.

Ashok- Yes Officer.

Policeman- You bought the house in that colony right?

Ashok- Yes officer.

Policeman- For how much did you get it?

Ashok- 45 lakhs.

Policeman- Do you have the property papers?

Ashok- No, the registration was in a few days.

Policeman- Do you have the contact information of the previous owner?

Ashok- Yes, Yes.

Policeman- Can you make a call?

Ashok- Yes.

Ashok called the previous owner but the call failed.

Policeman-Sir give me the number.

Ashok gave the number to the policeman and the policeman transferred the number for verification.

Policeman-Sir I don't know to whom had you given the money and got the keys but I want to tell you that the colony has been abandoned since 5 years and no one has gone there, even we fear going there .

Ashok- What!?

Policeman- Yes Sir.

Suddenly a message came on Ashok's Phone Your A/c is credited with ₹45,00,000.

Ashok- Sir, Sir my A/c is credited with 45 Lakhs.

Policeman- What ? give me the details.

Ashok transferred the details to the Policeman and the policeman transferred the details for verification.

After a few moments the policeman got a call.

Control Room- The number has been closed for 5 years and the bank account was also closed right there after the transaction, we are unable to get the details.

Policeman- Ok keep trying, I am interrogating the victims.

The policeman hung up the call and started interrogating others. He listened to everyone's experience and was shocked.

Policeman- I can't believe what my ears heard, it doesn't seem real, have you found something?

Control Room- No. Nothing we are investigating; you also go and report to the crime scene.

Policeman- Ok.

Chapter 19

Everyone was discharged from the hospital and they all went to their home and took Ashok with them.

Manohar- Who knew that this would happen to us, I still can't believe what happened to us. Now let's just forget everything and live a normal life.

Ashok- I am also flying back; my flight is tomorrow.

Manohar- You are leaving and you haven't told me?

Ashok- Everything happened so fast that I forgot to tell.

Manohar- You are right, but what about your luggage?

Ashok- I am taking nothing with me, all my items are in that house, it is sealed and I don't want to go back there.

Manohar- It is like a nightmare for all of us now, Sushma and Chetan both are very afraid, I hope we all get back to our normal lives soon.

Chapter 20

The Next Morning everyone gathered around the table for Breakfast but their faces said something else...

Manohar, Ashok, Chetan and Sushma everyone was still in shock thinking about what had happened to them. Manohar's parents were also disturbed and confused and were unable to believe the stories that were told to them about the incident. Suddenly the doorbell rang ting tong ting tong. Manohar got up and opened the door there was a police officer.

Manohar- Good Morning Sir.

Policeman- Good Morning, I brought your friend's baggage and passport.

Manohar- Oh! Thank you, sir please come inside, let's have breakfast.

Policeman- No No, I can't actually I have to go to the investigation site, but thank you for asking.

Manohar- Oh! ok sir.

Manohar closed the door and sat on the chair.

Manohar- Ashok your passport and baggage is here.

Ashok- That's good, I have my flight today at 4:30 PM, Manohar can you drop me to the airport at 1:30 PM ?

Manohar- Yes, I will.

Suddenly another doorbell rang. Manohar got up and opened the door, it was the delivery boy.

Delivery Boy- Good Morning sir, Here is your order.

Manohar took the order, made the payment, and kept the breakfast on the table and everyone started having it.

After breakfast, everyone talked a little bit and calmed each other. The time was 1 PM.

Ashok- Manohar I think we should leave now.

Manohar- Have you checked everything?

Ashok- Yes.

Ashok said goodbye to everyone, took blessings from Manohar's Parents, and left for the airport.

Chapter 21

After dropping Ashok went to his work.

At home, like on normal days, Sushma started doing her household chores and Chetan was watching TV, they all resumed their normal routines.

At night Manohar came home, everyone had dinner and went to sleep.

In the early morning at 3 AM Sushma heard a sound coming from the kitchen, she went to check and found that it was Chetan.

Sushma- What are you doing here? It's 3 AM!

Chetan- I was looking for something to eat.

Sushma- Why didn't you sleep yet.

Chetan- I was unable to, whenever I try to, everything comes in front and that black spirit is also coming into my dreams.

Sushma- Don't worry everything will be back to normal soon.

Chetan- Yes Mata Shri.

Sushma- You want apple?

Chetan- No Mata Shri, I am going to sleep.

Sushma- Ok beta Good Night.

Chetan- Good Night, Mata Shri.

Sushma and Chetan both went to their rooms to sleep.

Chapter 22

Everyone woke up like normal mornings.

Manohar and his father had breakfast and left for work. Sushma woke Chetan at noon Chetan woke up restless.

Sushma- You are looking tired.

Chetan- Yes, I am restless.

Sushma- Didn't you get proper sleep?

Chetan- No, I got to sleep only at 9 in the morning.

Sushma- Why? Because of Nightmares ?

Chetan- Yes.

Sushma- Don't worry everything will be back to normal soon.

Chapter 23

Manohar and his father were returning from work when they found that their regular way was under construction, so they had to take a very dark way, it was the only way. When they were going that way suddenly a strange person came in front of the car, Manohar was unable to stop the car and when he looked back it was the same black spirit. They both got afraid and rushed to their home. When they reached they were very scared.

Sushma- What happened Manohar !?

Manohar- We saw that! We saw that!

Sushma- WHAT?

Manohar- That Black Spirit.

Sushma- What!?

Manohar- Yes.

Sushma- What's happening with us ?

Manohar- I think we should leave it, it might be our disbelief.

Sushma- But.....

Manohar- Just Leave it and let's have dinner.

Sushma- Ok.

Chapter 24

It was 2:47AM, and Chetan felt like someone was calling his name.

Unknown Voice- Chetan...Chetan... Chetan

Chetan opened his eyes but was unable to move and speak.

Chetan got sleep paralysed A little light was coming into the room from the door, Chetan felt like someone was standing in front of his bed.

Unknown Voice- Chetan I can read your mind, you are wondering who I am. Did you forget me? We met last time at your uncle's house.

Chetan- The black spirit…. Help! Help! someone Help!

Black Spirit- Well you recognized me, don't worry, soon you and your family will be under my control, I will capture you all. By the way, no one can listen to you.

Chetan- What!?

Black Spirit- I think you should sleep now, my friend Chetan.

Chapter 25

In the Morning Sushma came and woke up Chetan

Sushma- Chetan beta wake up.

Chetan- Leave me. Leave me, help help !

Sushma- What happened Chetan, what are you doing? Why are you behaving like this?

Chetan- Where is the black spirit?

Sushma- You had another nightmare?

Chetan- It was not a nightmare this time, that spirit was standing in front of my bed, I got sleep paralyzed at that time, it was saying it would soon have control over all of us.

Sushma- It might be your other nightmare ?

Chetan- I hope it is.

Sushma- Let's go downstairs.

Chetan- Yes Mata Shri, where is Pita Shri ?

Sushma- He is at work.

Chetan- Ok

Chetan had breakfast and went back to his room.

He was thinking of what had happened to him last night when suddenly his phone rang.

जय हनुमान ज्ञान गुण सागर।

जय कपीस तिहुं लोक उजागर॥

रामदूत अतुलित बल धामा।

अंजनि-पुत्र पवनसुत नामा॥

It was his friend Rohan.

Chetan- Hi bro how are you?

Rohan- I am good bro but you don't sound good, what happened?

Chetan- Nothing bro, you tell, you called after so long.

Rohan- Yes bro, I called you a few nights back, remember, when you had to visit your uncle's house

Chetan- Oh yes, I remember .

Rohan- Yes, that day I called you to tell you that I won't be available for a few days because I am going on a trip.

Chetan- Oh! How was your trip?

Rohan- It was good, you tell me how was your dinner at your Uncle's new house?

After listening to this Chetan got a throwback of what happened with him.

Chetan- Rohan, I will call you in a bit.

Rohan- Ok Bro.

Chetan hung up the call After cutting the call Chetan felt malaise, Chetan started overthinking what if whatever that black spirit said came true, Chetan was getting depressed, he was getting stressed.

Chapter 26

When Sushma came upstairs to talk to Chetan she saw that he was sitting on the bed, his eyes were red, he was only looking straight toward the wall.

Sushma- Chetan are you ok?

Chetan didn't give any response Sushma was terrified, so she took Chetan and rushed to the doctor. She was so much stressed that in the way she almost crashed the car 3-4 times, but Chetan did not react.

When Sushma reached the hospital Chetan was immediately taken to the doctor's room.

After examining Chetan the Doctor came out.

Doctor- Who has come with Mr. Chetan?

Sushma- Doctor I am Chetan's mother, how is he? Is he ok now?

Doctor- Yes, he is alright now, I have given him a sleep injection and he is sleeping now.

Sushma- Thank God, doctor what happened to him?

Doctor- Was he in some sort of stress or something?

Sushma- No doctor.

Doctor- Was he able to get enough sleep?

Sushma- For 2-3 days he was not able to sleep properly.

Doctor- Keep his calm don't show any stress around him and make sure he gets enough sleep.

Sushma- Ok doctor.

Doctor- Pay the bill at the counter and then you can take him back.

Sushma- Ok doctor.

Sushma paid the bill and then took Chetan back home.

Chapter 27

When Chetan woke up, he found himself on the sofa.

Chetan- Where am I? How did I come here ? I was in my room.

Sushma- Calm down. Chetan calm down.

Suddenly the main door of the house opened, Manohar opened the door, and he and his father were very terrified.

Sushma- What happened, why did you open the door like that ? And why are you panting?

Manohar's Mom- What happened? Are you both ok?

Manohar- Nothing is right, we all are not safe.

Sushma- What? What are you saying ?

Manohar's Mom- What happened.

Manohar- Today when I and Pita Shri reached our office, Pita Shri went inside and I noticed a dent in front of the car, I picked up the dash cam and went inside, attached the dash cam to my laptop, while I was checking the footage I found nothing, then I remembered that a few days back I had seen a black spirit on our way back, but when I looked back there was nothing so out of curiosity I checked the footage of that day too when I played that footage I was shocked, I didn't believe my eyes, I replayed that footages few times and then I rushed back to our house.

Sushma- What we will do now?

Chetan- That spirit that I saw, whatever that said will come true.

Manohar- Which spirit? What did you see? What did it say?

Chetan told everything that happened to him to Manohar and others.

Manohar- I think we should call Pandit Ji and ask him for the solution.

Everyone agreed with Manohar. Manohar called Pandit Ji.

Manohar- Namaste Pandit Ji.

Pandit Ji- Namaste.

Manohar- Pandit Ji can you come to our house tomorrow?

Pandit Ji- Yes.

Manohar- Can you come around 12 PM ?

Pandit Ji- Yes I can come.

Manohar- Ok Pandit Ji.

Manohar Hung up the call.

Chapter 28

The next day everyone was ready before 12PM because Pandit Ji was coming to their home.

Manohar- It's already 12:15 and Pandit Ji didn't come yet.

The doorbell rang, Manohar opened the door and it was Pandit Ji.

Manohar- Namaste Pandit Ji.

Pandit Ji- Namaste.

Pandit Ji came inside and sat on the sofa.

Pandit Ji- Why have you called me?

Manohar told Pandit Ji about everything that happened with them during the past few days.

Pandit Ji- That's a very serious matter; can you show me the video of your dashcam?

Manohar- Yes Pandit Ji.

Manohar showed the video to Pandit Ji.

Pandit Ji- Tomorrow I will do some rituals.

Manohar- Ok Pandit Ji.

Chapter 29

The next day Pandit Ji came with things that were needed for the rituals Pandit Ji gathered everyone in the main lobby and started with the rituals. Pandit Ji threw some flowers on the floor as a part of the ritual and the flowers turned black as soon as they touched the ground, everyone's faces turned pale.

Pandit Ji- There is too much negative energy in your house and the spirit is taking over your house.

Manohar- WHAT!?

Chetan- Whatever that spirit said is coming true.

Manohar- Pandit Ji please tell me a solution.

PanditJi- To stop the spirit from taking over your house I will do a Hawan but it will only stop the spirit for a temporary period.

Manohar- Pandit ji isn't there a permanent solution?

Pandit Ji-There is.

Manohar- What is the solution ?

Pandit Ji- We have to go and perform rituals at the place from where this all started.

Manohar- WHAT!?

Pandit Ji- Yes, first let's secure the house.

Manohar- Yes Pandit ji.

Manohar and Pandit Ji went and brought all the necessary items that were needed for the ritual and started doing the hawan. In between the weird sounds started coming.

Manohar- From where are these sounds coming, should I go and check?

Pandit Ji- Don't go anywhere from here till the Hawan is complete, the spirit is trying to distract us.

Manohar- Ok. Pandit Ji.

The Hawan was almost on the end stage when the spirit came in front of everyone.

Black Spirit- Stop everything or no one will stay alive.

Pandit Ji- Just ignore it, it can't harm us.

Pandit Ji said this and started again the spirit started screaming and finally disappeared.

Pandit Ji- The Hawan is complete, Now your house is safe and the spirit cannot harm you for a few days.

Manohar- Thank you, Pandit ji.

Pandit Ji- Now tell me from where did all this start ?

Manohar told the full story to Pandit Ji.

Pandit Ji- Ok, now I understand.

Manohar- Pandit Ji now when do we have to go to that colony ?

Pandit Ji- As soon as possible where is your friend whom you visited? Is he safe?

Chapter 30

After listening to Pandit Ji Manohar immediately called Ashok. Someone else picked up the call.

The person on call- Whose this?

Manohar- Hi I'm Ashok's friend Manohar can you give him the phone?

The Person on call- Don't you know?

Manohar- What ?

The Person on call- A few days back he was found dead in his apartment, the investigations are still ongoing , and the cause of death has not been identified yet.

After listening to this Manohar's phone fell from his hands and he went through an emotional breakdown, everyone was shocked to see why Manohar was crying.

Sushma- What happened why are you crying?

Chetan- What happened Pita Shri ?

Manohar's Mom- What happened beta ?

Manohar's Dad- What happened ?

Manohar- Ashok-Ashok-Ashok is no more.

Everyone was shocked.

Pandit Ji- Sorry to interrupt, but this is the work of none other than that of the spirit.

Chapter 31

Manohar wiped his tears and stood up.

Manohar- Pandit Ji can we go today to the colony?

Pandit Ji- It's not possible, we have to collect the necessary items too.

Manohar- Pandit Ji let's go and collect the necessary items and then we both will go and end the chapter of the Spirit.

Pandit Ji- We both cannot go to the colony alone, everyone who was present in the colony when you visited your friend's house has to be present there.

Manohar- You mean Sushma and Chetan also have to be their?

Pandit Ji- Yes.

Manohar- Ok, tomorrow night we will get rid of that spirit.

Chapter 32

The Next day in the evening Pandit Ji came to Manohar's house with things that were required for the rituals.

Manohar- Namaste Pandit Ji.

Pandit Ji- Namaste.

Manohar- Come inside.

Pandit Ji went inside and sat on the sofa.

Pandit Ji- Is everyone ready?

Manohar- Yes Pandit ji, we will leave in a bit.

Pandit Ji- Ok.

A few minutes later Sushma and Chetan came into the lobby.

Sushma- Namaste Pandit Ji.

Chetan- Namaste Pandit Ji.

Pandit Ji- Namaste.

Manohar- I think we should leave now.

Sushma- Let's Go.

Manohar's Parents also came in the lobby.

Manohar's Mother- Are you guys leaving for the colony?

Manohar- Yes Mata Ji.

Manohar's Mother- Take care beta.

Manohar's Father- Take care beta.

Manohar, Sushma, and Chetan touched Manohar's parents' feet, took their blessings and they all left for the Colony.

Chapter 33

On the way everyone was very worried, Manohar's parents were also calling them to give them support. When they arrived near the colony everyone started to build their confidence.

Manohar- We have arrived.

Pandit Ji- Let's go.

Everyone came out of the car, Pandit Ji took the items and everyone stood in front of the gate. The entrance was sealed with yellow tapes by the police They crossed the tapes and went inside They were standing at the entrance and looking at the colony. They were getting throwbacks of what they faced.

Pandit Ji- We have to perform the rituals in front of the house.

Manohar- Ok Pandit Ji, Let's go there.

Everyone started walking towards their destination and a sudden voice came from back giving them chills.

Unknown Voice- What were you all thinking, you will come into my area and defeat me like you all did before? No, you all were wrong, you were all able to defeat me because that wasn't my place but now you are in my colony and now I won't let you go alive.

Manohar- That spirit, it is here, we have to do our work fast.

They all started running towards the house but the spirit suddenly came in front of them and they all stop but Pandit ji took Ganga Jal in his hands and splashed it on the spirit and the spirit disappeared.

Pandit Ji- We have to perform the rituals in front of the house.

Manohar- Ok Pandit ji, let's go there.

Everyone started walking towards their destination and a sudden came from back giving them chills

They all started running towards the house but the spirit suddenly came in front of them and they all stopped Pandit Ji took Ganga Jal in his hands and splashed it on the spirit and the spirit disappeared.

They started running again towards the house. They went a little further when they saw Manohar's father lying on the ground.

Manohar- Pita Ji

Manohar immediately ran toward his father and tried to wake him up.

Manohar- Pita Ji wake up, wake up, what happened to you?

Pandit Ji- Manohar leave him, he is not your father, it's just a distraction caused by the spirit to stop us, get aside from him.

Manohar got aside and Pandit Ji splashed Ganga Jal on the body and it turned to dust.

Pandit Ji- I told you it was just a distraction.

They all started running again and then they saw their destination.

Manohar- We are almost there, let's keep running.

Suddenly several spirits surrounded them, all the spirits were slowly coming toward them.

Chetan- What's happening?

Manohar- Pandit Ji what will we do now ?

Pandit Ji- This all is just an illusion, everyone should hold each other's hands, close your eyes, and just run.

Everyone did what Pandit Ji said and the next movement they were out. Then they rushed and reached their destination. Suddenly Chetan stabbed Manohar in his foot.

Manohar- Aah! Aah! Help! Help!

Chetan (Spirit)- Hahahahahaha, you all can't beat me.

The Spirit made everyone unconscious.

Chapter 34

Everyone woke up and found themselves in a room

Sushma- Where are we?? Manohar are you ok??

Manohar- No not at all.

Pandit Ji- I think we are trapped in a room.

Sushma- Yes, but where is Chetan !?

Pandit Ji- The spirit might have hidden him somewhere, we have to look for him, first let's get out of here.

Sushma got up and tried to open the door, but the door didn't open.

Pandit Ji - Let me try.

Pandit Ji also trid opening the door but he was also unsuccessful in his attempt.

Pandit Ji - This door has got locked by some spells.

Pandit Ji performed a small ritual and the door opened. Sushma tore the arm of her top and tied

Manohar's wound with it. Sushma helped Manohar get up and they all went out of the room, they all found that they all were in the same house but on the first floor, they all went down the stairs and reached the main lobby, and what they saw there was shocking, Chetan was lying on the floor and some ritual was being performed him.

Sushma- Chetannnnn !!

Black Spirit- You guys got up very soon, my ritual was almost complete.

Pandit Ji - Now you will never be able to complete it.

Pandit Ji chanted and threw a holy white powder on the spirit, and the spirit disappeared. Pandit ji splashed some Ganga jal on Chetan's face and he woke up.

Sushma- Chetan beta are you ok ?

Chetan- Yes Mata Shri.

Pandit Ji- We have only this time, we should start the rituals.

Manohar- Ok Pandit ji.

When everyone was leaving the house, a hand appeared from the floor and caught Pandit Ji's feet and the spirit tied him with its spells and everyone stopped there and the spirit captured everyone, suddenly a phone rang-

जय हनुमान ज्ञान गुण सागर।

जय कपीस तिहुं लोक उजागर॥

रामदूत अतुलित बल धामा।

अंजनि-पुत्र पवनसुत नामा॥

Spirit disappeared and everyone got freed everyone ran out and Pandit Ji started his rituals and then they started doing the hawan.

Pandit Ji- Let's do it quickly.

Pandit Ji started doing the hawan. The spirit came in front of them.

Black Spirit- You thought you could harm me. hahahahahha.

Spirit tried to come near them and harm them but it was unsuccessful in its attempts.

Pandit Ji- I have created a pure layer around us, you cannot come inside and harm us.

The Hawan was almost complete, the spirit also started screaming and then disappeared, and the Hawan was complete. Everyone was happy and were still not able to believe what they had faced in a few days. Everyone walked towards the car and there was a page stuck in the windshield wipers, everyone ignored it and sat in the car and Sushma started driving.

Chetan- Mata Shri why are you driving? What happened to Pita Shri?

Sushma- You Stabbed his foot.

Chetan- Nice joke Mata Shri now tell me the real reason.

Manohar showed his foot to Chetan.

Chetan- WHAT happened to you, Pita Shri ??

Sushma- He got stabbed.

Chetan- Who stabbed him ??

Sushma- You Chetan you.

Chetan- Why I will stab him.

Sushma then told Chetan everything that happened to them.

Sushma- Chetan who had called you up when we were caught by the spirit?

Chetan- Mata Shri it was Rohan, he saved us.

Manohar- Your best friend saved us.

Chapter 35

Everyone reached home at 8 AM, when they entered Manohar's parents were waiting for them in the lobby, they all met and were very happy They took Pandit Ji's blessings and Pandit Ji left for his home.

Sushma- Now we can get a good sleep.

Manohar- Yes.

Chetan- No more nightmares finally !!

They all went to their rooms to sleep.

Chapter 36

At about 5 PM Chetan's phone Rang

जय हनुमान ज्ञान गुण सागर।

जय कपीस तिहुं लोक उजागर॥

रामदूत अतुलित बल धामा।

अंजनि-पुत्र पवनसुत नामा॥

It was Rohan's call.

Rohan- Hi bro.

Chetan- Hi.

Rohan- Want to go and eat something?

Chetan- Yes bro let's go.

Rohan came and picked up Chetan from his home On the way a black cat crossed their way.

Chetan- Stop Stop Stop.

Rohan- Why What happened ??

Chetan- A black cat crossed the way.

Rohan- So why did you ask me to stop? You only told me that you don't believe in these types of myths, ghosts etc.

Chetan- But now I believe.

Rohan- Hahahahaha what happened to you in a few days ?

Chetan- Nothing just leave it and take another way.

Rohan- Ok bro.

Chetan- By the way Rohan you saved me.

Rohan- Bro. How?

Chetan- Nothing -Nothing, bro you tell me why had you called me last night?

Rohan- I wanted to tell an incident that happened with me, a few days back when I called you you suddenly hung up the call, I went to Ria's colony alone I passed twice in front of her house, when the 3rd time her father almost caught me, I drove the scooter on full speed and escaped, I was very afraid, last night I called to tell you this only.

Chetan- Oh, it was very dangerous.

Rohan- Yes bro.

After eating Rohan dropped Chetan back home.

The next day when Manohar and his father were leaving for work, Manohar saw the page still stuck between windshield wipers, he picked up the paper and started reading it. He was extremely shocked after reading it. He immediately ran inside his house and called everyone in the lobby.

What Manohar saw in the Paper was-

The Story Of The Colony

The place where this colony was built, before there was an abandoned graveyard. One day a builder came and finalised the location for building the colony here. He gave a petition for the location but was rejected several times, but the builder had links with politicians and thus he got his petition approved. The construction started, many paranormal activities happened but the builder didn't care about it. The day when the houses were listed for sale, every house got sold within minutes, but those who bought the houses in the colony were found dead in the place where they were living before. The builder got to know that he had done something very terrible and might have triggered the spirits or something. He used his connections and got the cases closed; he knew that no one would ask for an investigation because all the families were killed. The builder also left the country thinking that he would be safe there, but he was wrong, after shifting abroad he was found dead in his house and

www.ingramcontent.com/pod-product-compliance
Lightning Source LLC
LaVergne TN
LVHW041542070526
838199LV00046B/1794